A Collection of Unique Short Stories

Collection of Unique Short Stories

Short Stories, Volume 1

Mark Reed

Published by Mark Reed, 2024.

This is a work of fiction. Similarities to real people, places, or events are entirely coincidental.

COLLECTION OF UNIQUE SHORT STORIES

First edition. December 26, 2024.

Copyright © 2024 Mark Reed.

ISBN: 979-8230287902

Written by Mark Reed.

Table of Contents

For all the people who got me to where I am

6 Word Stories

MARK REED

Hospital arrival
Doctor arrives
Diagnosis Found

Children's giggle
Lightened faces
Laughter ensues

She left him
His life began

Sixtieth year
Look back
Life lived

Her beauty
Is told
Many ways

Writer agonies
Story created
Journey begins

Universe so large
Makes us small

Radio plays
Disembodied voice
Emptiness filled

I told you
I was sick

On the dancefloor
We dance together

Things will
Work out
One day

Her love
It came
with conditions

His wrinkles
Can tell
Many stories

The homeless person
Can teach many

Your life
Too short
To waste

Why follow
When you
Can lead?

The giant leads
protecting the child

The mermaid sun-bakes
Her tail glistening

The monster awakes
Town's people protected

The planet looms
Long mission complete

The lover awakes
True love found

The robot pilot
Trusted with craft

Australian outback
Dreamtime stories
Ancient past

I'll guide
He said
path uncertain

The Angel walked
Beside the traveller

A ministry of equality
Welcomes all

Do not question
All great teaching

Her curves alluring
Her hugs divine

Superhero girl
Defeats the enemy again

Early dawn
First light
Day begins

Indigenous Australians
First people
Dreamtime stories

Family tree
Stories from the past

Another day
What will I learn

Baby born
A life started anew

Another year
What will I discover

Space exploration
To search
To discover

The artist struggles
Does captures images

Motorcycle riding

Traversing winding
mountain roads

Starting anew
Leaving old life behind

Egyptian times
Pharaohs rule
Pyramids built

Nervous Poet prepares.
Grateful applause received

She smiles
With plenty
Of joy

I'm writing
To make
A difference

He doubted
His abilities
Others didn't

He rejoiced loudly
Because he could

Hospital ghost
Comes when
She's needed

Your children
A treasure
To behold

Your age
Is just
A number

Rapunzel, tower bound
Long hair escape

Midwinter time
Chill air
Frosty mornings

Dragon launches
From the highest mountain

Her love
For him
Is real

100 Word Stories

C lara the Mischievous Leprechaun

Living amongst the meadows beauty lives Clara the Mischievous Leprechaun, known for her beauty, and her hypnotic songs. She is the essence of mischief itself.

It is believed by those who seek her hair, holds magical powers. If a strand you find good fortune, your way will for ever follow.

She lives in that place other legendary creatures dwell; it is a place known only to them, but if you find you will be mystified, it is a place you must never find.

So the next time mischief comes your way expect to hear her singing her songs of mischief.

IMAGINE IF ROMEO AND Juliet hated each other?

Imagine if Romeo started fighting with Juliet, instead of it being a beautiful love story. It's a story of opposing teenagers, that instead of wonderful poetic words, we read words of aggression.

If Romeo went after Juliet, throwing her over his shoulder, and gave her a spanking instead of giving her a cuddle, what would her reaction be?

And the final death scene is a wrestling match. How would the play end?

If Romeo and Juliet be a story of now, just how would that story go? Would it be a story of war, or of a huge arms dealer?

THE BAR IN OUTER SPACE

On a foreign planet, in a sacred building, lays the bar in outer space.

A segregated bar, only males can drink there, the drinks are too dangerous for their woman.

Gathering, they discuss life on their planet, and the troubles of their partners and children. They curse their leaders and their employers too, as another round of drinks is served.

The solemnity of the drinking here is legendary among the other planets, whose beings travel to experience and to drink at a bar famous throughout the universe.

The meals they serve are legendary to, found nowhere else but here.

THE NIGHT OF THE SPECIAL dance

Saira Elmboots the beautiful woodland fairy with wings like lace steps delicately on the waterlily, as she waits for her partner to arrive.

Nimbus Beechcone, the majestic frog upon seeing her approaches with delight. For tonight, under the light of the full moon, they will dance the sacred lily pond dance.

As others watch and the music plays, they dance majestically upon the lily. What a beautiful sight for those who are seeing it. It is held only once a year.

As the moonlight drops, the dance end;. They part only to meet again, when the dance their sacred dance.

THE FINAL RIDE

The rain falls harder against his blue motorcycle helmet, to reach his children his only goal.

Lightning flashes, thunder roars and yet he continues to ride, because he knows they'll be waiting to hug him tight the moment he steps through the door.

Cheers ring out, a nervous mother and wife wait, her nervousness not showing on her face, because she knows the perils her husband is facing.

Lightning bolts light up the perilous road, lighting up what appears like a small ocean of before him.

The final run, the last few streets now, his house appears before him.

home.

THE IMPRISONED PRINCESS

On a distant planet, the princess is imprisoned in a dome, on a foreign planet who atmosphere is dangerous. The princess waits to be freed.

A rocket is being prepared to launch the rescue mission on her home planet.

To be wed to their prince, to be the mother of his children is the dream of those who kidnapped her.

Four days in space is how they need to travel to rescue the imprisoned princess, so prepare they do a vicious enemy is waiting, a ferocious battle awaits.

Across the planet they battle the enemy, her rescue their ultimate goal.

THE FINAL MEAL

We greet each other before taking our places as memories of that special night return, when things did change for the better we thought, it was the night that changed it all.

I remember the nights when my work meant I had to spend time away from her, but then return to a welcoming meal, of a life I hoped to live.

But change did come and the feelings to, our life was coming undone.

So now I sit and reminisce of a life that ended all too soon, as alone I eat remembering those times wondering what's to come.

THE LETTER

Finding a mysterious letter in the drawer of a cabinet, I take it out as I wonder what it could be.

Is it a secret message, or something from long ago?

Could it be an impassioned love letter, a call from a shattered heart?

Has it been taken from a place of secrets? Is it the words of royalty long ago? What is the reason for the seal? Is it hiding a secret curse?

If I was to break the seal, what is it I could find? Precious photos, an ancient message. Could it hold the map to a secret treasure?

THE MERMAID DANCE

Through the waves and under the sea, the Mermaid begins her dance.

Beneath the ships, as they sail by, the beautiful dance begins.

If seen by humans, they would not understand, because how can something so beautiful live beneath the crashing waves, but live they do beside the many fish that fill the many oceans?

Rare it is they are seen in small streams, for their existence must remain hidden, because if found by humans they would certainly be hunted, their secret would be no more.

But loved by those who believe in true beauty, of the mysteries that exist.

THE PERFECT NIGHT

Taking her in my arms, I tenderly stroke her luscious hair as it cascades down her back.

The allure of her perfume signals in me a night of passion, of unbridled sensuality, a night we will not forget.

To the couch we head, our house is silent, photos reminding us of what we have, our four precious children, the source of our joy, but tonight there is silence.

For tonight they wind my parents around their fingers, the start of a weekend for us, to celebrate that day we committed ourselves to each other, of a life I never imagined.

THE HAUNTED BOOKCASE

Ascending the staircase she arrives at the grand bookcase, an ancient house with many memories, *'This is the book you want,'* the voice from the bookcase said, as a hand pushed out a book, Gulliver's Travels was the book that was selected, a book about a grand story.

With the book in her hand, she descends again as she prepares to read the story.

She wonders as she reads could she go on such a journey, to arrive at a place where she would be a giant.

To journey again and find other places, places unlike she has ever experienced.

500 Word Stories

Echoes of Yesterday

Stepping inside the time machine, hoping to arrive somewhere around the start of 1970, Nick Adams secures his harness.

Flicking all the necessary switches, he notices the time gauge reads 2128.

He knows from his training it's vitally important for him to arrive at the appointed date. He must flick the yellow switch first, followed by the red and then the green.

But a last-minute order from central control cause him to flick the red switch first followed by the green and then the yellow.

Realising his mistake, he attempts to turn the abort lever, but instead of it shutting down, the machine begins to buzz.

'Where the hell am I?' he thinks to himself as the machine slowly shuts down, looking over at the time gauge, he sees that it's showing 1992, opening the door, he sees the machine has landed in what appears to be an abandon building, realising he landed in a time when a lot of

suspicion regarding aliens caused people to do extraordinary things he located a shop selling the latest in men's wear.

Emerging from the building his time machine landed in, he stepped onto the street, and noticed that the clothes he wore were unlike those of the surrounding people, searching for a store selling clothes bought clothes that will help him blend in.

Investigation and return within six months were the primary orders he was working under, but as he walked along, he wondered if six months was going to be long enough for the scientist's needs.

Finding a place to live, he one day discovered he had established a relationship with a lady named Lucy, a lady he felt he had always known, their connection was like none he had ever experienced before, and he started to wonder if this was the place and time he was supposed to live.

"What do you mean you're from the future?" Lucy asked, after divulging the truth after a spirited evening in bed.

"I realise it's hard to believe, but I'm actually from 2128?"

"And people from that time, time travel do they?" she asked, trying to comprehend what she had been told.

"No, only scientists like me."

"So, are you intending to head back there?"

"I can't see that I can now that I have met you. I don't want to ruin what we've got."

With Lucy by his side, he re-entered into the building nine months since his arrival, only to discover a message on the main screen reading, '*Your mission is overdue, it's imperative you return.*'

"What are you going to do?" she asks hoping he's not intending to leave her, "Do what they want."

Buying a mannequin at a local thrift store, he slips on his uniform, placing in the top pocket a series of photos, and a note reading, '*Mission successful, I arrived in the year 1992 where I met a lady I have strong affection for, refuse to abandon her,*' he flicks a switch, before shutting the door.

PUZZLE OF LOVE

Home to two people with unspoken love is Willow Creek, renowned for its majestic ghost gum and scenic beauty.

Anne-Marie, a lady with long dark hair, passionately photographs the creatures frequently seen in the tree's branches, while her dear friend, Andrew, a man with a thick bushy beard, is engaged in a spirited competition to photograph elusive animals that sometimes appear there.

As bad as each other when it comes to telling the other how they feel, confides with their friend Margaret, who often wants to knock their heads together after telling each of them to go and see a movie or to share a meal.

"Look, the chicken take away you both like is advertising a meal for two," she said to the nervous Andrew, "why don't you get one and then invite Anne-Marie over to share it with you?"

"Do you think I should?"

"What have you got to lose," she said as she held his face between her hands, "She's not likely to leave you now.

Standing beside her taking photos of a colourful parrot sitting in the branches of the tree, Andrew lowers his camera as he asks, "I've heard our favourite chicken take away is advertising a meal for two, would you like to share one with me?"

Lowering her camera, a puzzled Anne-Marie faced him as she asked, "When?"

"Next Saturday, and before you ask, at my place."

Like an electric charge coursing through them, they both changed into what they considered to be their finest outfits, with a passion for all things old, Anne-Marie put on a beautiful old-style off the shoulder flowing white dress, while Andrew put on a white shirt, grey vest and light brown tailcoat.

Returning after buying what he hoped was going to be the best meal either of them had ever enjoyed, he placed them on ornate dishes. Anne-Marie walked through the door.

"I love that dress you're wearing."

"I love your outfit too. Thank you!"

It was as if they had been married for years as they shared their meal. "I've never enjoyed anything before in my life," Anne-Marie said as she enjoyed the wine Andrew had served with the meal.

"Thank you, it was recommended to me."

"How would you feel about posing for me?"

"What do you have in mind?" Anne-Marie asked, wondering what was on his mind.

"Honestly, what you're happy with?"

"Are you talking about me posing nude?"

"Only if you're happy with it," he said, his head spinning with the possibilities.

"It's actually something I've been wanting to do since I met you. I just didn't know how to ask you?"

Like a wall collapsing, Anne-Maries secret came to life.

Posing in more seductive poses than he could've imagined she posed as he captured her naked image.

"Nobody's going to see these but us," she said as she slipped on a gown.

"These are our secret poses."

"Now let me do you," she said, shocking Andrew, a mischievous expression on her face.

THE GREAT AIRSHIP RACE

Twirling his handlebar moustache between his fingers, the very egotistical Sabastian Thompkins, the Mayor of Granville Crossing, announced to the very headstrong Sarah Sterling, "Airships are a thing made and flown only by men."

Beside her, a picture of the first man to use a lightweight airship to scale the lofty peaks of Iron back mountain, the man who flew the colossal airship, and the picture of the man who set an airspeed record using an airship, the only picture missing was of her, the first woman to have built and flown an airship.

"How many times have I got to tell you, women do not have the mental proficiency to build such a complicated craft?"

"How can you say that?" her eyes bulging with rage, "when I've already built and flown my own airship?"

"I will not hear another word about it," he says as he waved her off, angering her.

"YOU'RE FORGETTING, they think a woman is only here to run a house, and raise children," Lavina, Sarah's mother said.

"I know what you're capable of. You just need to convince them."

"How?" she asks, frustrated.

"By winning the Great Airship Race."

She knew her mother was right. She just needed to convince the rest of the airship guild.

TO ENTER THE RACE, airships must be specifically designed and built for it. Over the years, many unusual designs have been entered, some of which have exploded or collapsed at the start line or during the race itself.

KNOWING WHAT WAS NEEDED, Cassandra, her chief engineer, and Sally and Debbie, renown airship makers, started to build what they hoped was going to be both a strong but lightweight airship.

Using a hanger which sits an adjacent to her workshop, and utilising the finest machinery and materials, the craft started to come to life.

In buildings around them, anxious airship builders got to work building what they hope is going to be a winning airship.

Plans were written and re-written as the final design is argued over, "But if we use this type of gondola, it'll mean we have more control over it, "Debbie says as she points to the blueprint."

"But if we use this type of tail wing, the craft will be more stable," Cassandra said as she pointed to the design she invented.

With the final design decided, and the airship built, they prepared for the race.

It was an incredible sight, airships of almost every shape and size lined up, all hoping for a successful race.

"Welcome everyone to today's Great Airship Race," Mayor Thompkins the race M.C. announced, "Fly straight, fly true.

Sarah was ecstatic to see she was the early leader, determine to stay there she turned her craft into the prevailing winds.

Flying faster than she had before, she sailed across the sky, the other airships trailing.

Seeing the finishing line, she lightened the ship, causing it to fly faster.

"We did it," she shouted as they passed the finishing line. Congratulations Sarah.

THE HAUNTED MIRROR

Walking down a cobblestone street, Elara Simpkins, a painter of the strange and unusual steps into an antique shop attracted by its many strange and unusual items.

Entering the shop, she sees a tall old-style mirror more beautiful than she had ever seen before.

She was enticed by the scent of aged wood, and as she looked at it, she wondered what stories it could tell.

'Come with me and I'll take you to a place where dragons can be seen from the tops of mighty mountains, where fairies can be seen flying among trees, and gnomes hurrying around the forest floor.'

Startled, Elara jumped back just as a beautiful woman appeared in the mirror.

'Take me to your place and I'll show you wondrous things.'

Good things began to change for Elara. Her paintings, once only the desire of those who enjoyed the odd and the strange started to appear in larger art galleries where people, who would have once mocked her works began to marvel at her style.

Asked to sell them by Andrew, a man who runs a gallery, she readily agreed with the paintings selling for more than she could ever imagine.

'I need you to paint the images I am showing you,' the voice said as a picture of olden times appeared in the mirror.

She saw men riding penny farthings beside others driving various shapes and sizes of horse-drawn vehicles.

There were women in elegant dresses, while others appeared as slaves of the front of what appeared to be 18th century buildings.

Erecting her easel, she sat at it as she painted the images that continued to appear in the mirror, like a film telling a story about the past.

Day and night Elara worked her hands cramping as she captured each image. After three days of solid work, the final painting was finished.

Exhibiting them at Andrew's gallery, she was surprised to hear many of the people say this or that painting was of their relative, before buying them.

Returning home, Elara went up to the mirror asking, "What have you done to me?"

'I got you to capture a time in those people's lives. Tell me, did they buy them?'

Surprised at this question, she replied, "They did."

As time went on, more and more images began to appear on the screen, compelling Elara to paint until the last image was finished.

"Why is there only this one image of a lady I'm assuming is famous?"

'Almost famous sadly, I'm not sure of her name, but if things had been different, she would have been one of Australia's famous actresses.'

Knowing the importance of capturing this image, Elara started to get to work.

Capturing the shine in her eyes, the pink of her cheeks, and the beauty of her long golden hair, Elara finally finished.

"Who's this?' Andrew asked when Elara put it on display.

"Oh my goodness!" this lady said when she first saw the painting, "This is my Grandmother Katherine."

WHITEHAVEN FARM

When James Reynolds died tragically in a horse-riding accident, his daughter, Paige, a lady with waist-length auburn hair, inherited Whitehaven Farm.

Managing the farm on her own at first felt like scaling the highest mountain, but as time went on, she found she could do it on her own.

One day she was startled by a wanderer, Tom, a man with rough brown hair wearing damaged bib and brace overalls looking for work.

At first Paige was reluctant to help him, but as time went on, and the story of why he became a wander emerged, her resolve lessened, and Tom went from sleeping rough in the shed to sharing her bed.

Tom found it hard to relax around Paige, but as days turned into weeks, and they turned into months, the connection between them grew, and Tom discovered, to his delight, Paige was with child.

"Oh know, what a time?" Tom said as the smoke of the approaching bush fire filled the sky.

Bigger than either of them had ever seen before, the fire destroyed all in its path.

"Now what?" a clearly upset Paige said.

"We rebuild and start again.

It was touch & go for a while, which was going to happen first, the house rebuild or Paige's baby's arrival, but a week after the last nail was hammered in, Tom rushed Paige to the hospital.

Smiles were infectious amongst the locals when they saw Paige and Tom push their baby, a girl they named Cassandra in the old-fashioned pram one of the firefighters gave them.

The birth of their second child, a boy three years later which both delighted but disgusted Cassandra when she discovered he was growing inside her mummy's tummy.

"Is he really in there?" Cassandra asked as she ran her hand across Paige's stomach.

"Yes, honey, can't you feel him?"

The day of his birth was a day of celebration for Cassandra, because in her words, he was finally someone she could play with.

Paige had always believed he was joking when Tom talked about installing a horizontal bungy, like a conventional bungy, but attached to a wall.

Paige was alarmed after spending a day in the city to hear their children appearing to be tortured.

Alarmed, she ran into the lounge room and saw their children pulling against giant bungies as they tried to reach their favourite teddy.

"What on earth have you done?"

"What I said I was going to do."

"Stop this. They're going to hurt themselves."

"What a load of rubbish. Look at their smiles."

Paige had never considered being a mother growing up, but as she watched Tom playing with them she knew that unlike a dog, she couldn't abandon them.

"Read them this," Tom said, realising she was having troubles. Sitting either side of her, they looked lovingly into her eyes as she read them their favourite nursery rhyme.

"That was fantastic mum," they both said before kissing her on the cheeks.

Short stories

Babbles Extraordinary Emporium

Babbles Emporium was known as the place where anything could be purchased.

From clothes to pet rocks, from computers of every type to book and magazines that couldn't be found anywhere else, and if a certain item was sought, they would go out of their way to get it.

Opened by the eccentric Paul and Gina Babbles in the Australian country town of Mossy Creek Ridge, it struggled to gain a name early on as they chased away the demons of earlier, poorly run emporiums.

Unsurprisingly, when Paul and Gina Babbles opened theirs scepticism was rife, many believing that they would operate the emporium in the same sloppy manner.

Love at First Sight

Since seeing a picture of a lady with knee-length hair when she was a little girl, Gina had been reluctant to have hers cut, only allowing her parents to have it trimmed so it wouldn't be in her eyes. When she was invited to attend the Mossy Creek Ridge Valentine's Day Dance, her light brown hair, which shone in the light, was already waist length. After washing it, she slowly plaited it into an intricate braid.

As Paul and his friends walked through the double wooden doors, they entered a room buzzing with excitement.

Paul had dressed in his favourite black three-piece suit, complete with black trousers, a mauve shirt, and the white bow tie gifted by his grandfather. He had planned to be the beau of the ball.

It didn't take him long to spot Gina as she stood at the far wall talking with her girlfriends.

Intrigued by her hair as it hung against her well-fitting black dress, he was taken by her magnificent large hazel eyes, highlighted by the most stunning eye liner. Her natural facial features were something to behold. Accentuated even more by subtle application of her make-up.

"Who's that cutie over there?" Paul asks his friends nervously as they stood against the opposite wall.

"That's Gina Higgins," Paul his best friend says. "word is she hasn't had her hair cut since she was a little girl. She's not stand-offish. Why don't you introduce yourself and blow her away with your incredible dancing skills?"

Uncharacteristically shy tonight, Paul was feeling as if he was walking through thick clay, making his way over to her.

"Good evening. My name is Paul. May I say you're looking very attractive?"

"Thank you Paul, my name is Gina." She took her hand in his and smiles warmly. "I rarely see men wearing a bow tie."

"This was a gift from my grandfather. All the men in my family have worn bow ties."

"I love when family traditions are carried on generation after generation."

"Would you do me the honour of dancing with me?"

"I would love to."

Joining the other couples on the dancefloor, Gina's hair brushed against Paul's hand as he placed it on her back and they began to dance.

"If you don't mind me asking, why is your hair as long as it is?"

"When I was around five years old, I was looking through one of my mother's fashion magazines. I had come upon a picture of this beautiful lady, whose hair ended at her knees. I never knew girls grew their hair that long. But after going through other magazines, I discovered many models wore their hair at least as long, if not longer. I decided there and then that I was going to grow my hair as long as I could.

"Well, it certainly is beautiful. Tell me, are you going to let it grow any longer?"

"I've always wanted to see how long it will grow. But if it grows beyond my feet, I have no choice but to trim it back."

"If you're free tomorrow, would you care to join me for lunch?"

Love Grows

The relationship between Paul and Gina steadily grew over the years. He would tell her tales about the raft of emporiums his grandparents used to take him to when he was a child.

Gina would tell him how she used to argue with her parents every time they wanted her to cut her hair.

"I always loved being taken to Smyths Emporium, in particular. I would always go to the shelf, the one that had the books about space travel and robots. I used to dream about travelling to Mars." Paul would say.

"I always knew when my parents weren't happy with my decision to never have my hair cut. Whenever either of them took me to our usual shopping centre, they always parked in the same area. I knew it was the closet one to the hairdresser they both used. I would turn feral if they got me anywhere near it. I threatened I would drop out of school if they had my hair cut." Gina's anecdotes always made Paul smile.

They were destined to marry. When they did, they were inspired to run an emporium of their own.

"We need to offer the townsfolk an emporium like no other. Fit for purpose and for the good of the people." Paul says.

He and Gina had scrimped and saved for years with this in mind. When the sad passing of Paul's grandparents left them stunned, they had no idea that Paul was to be bequeathed enough to complete their dreams.

Babbles Comes to Life

Purchasing an unflattering square black building in the centre of town which sat between two similarly unflattering buildings, they set about creating Babbles Emporium.

"In order to honour my grandparents, our emporium needs to standout. It needs to be the building people stop at whenever they drive down the street; whenever they walk down the street," Paul says as he and Gina stood across the road from their purchase.

Memories of Smyths Emporium flashed through Paul's mind, its stained-glass windows, curved roof, wide veranda, and the Penny Farthing Bike that stood out the front.

Having found a builder prepared to put a curved roof with a wide veranda onto the building, a glazier to put each letter of Babbles Emporium into individual panes that would sit on either side of the double wooden doors, accomplished the first stage of the project. Then there were the finishing touches, the purchase of a furphy water tank and a penny farthing bike. Both would sit between the building's uprights, Babbles Emporium was open.

The reputation of Babbles Emporium quickly spread. Soon, stories both fake and true flowed. People would say that they could buy the most incredible things at a price they could afford.

Before too long, Gina broke the news to Paul in her typical unsubtle way.

"Surprise, Paul. We have twins on the way," Gina says as if it were an everyday occurrence.

The twins would have an everlasting and positive effect on Gina and Paul, and indeed Babbles Emporium.

A Germ of an Idea

Remembering the story Paul used to tell her about sitting in Smyths Emporium reading books about space travel and robots, Gina imagined opening a part of the emporium for a children's story reading group.

It needs to be a place they'll enjoy coming to. She thinks to herself, imagining their children sitting amongst the others as they enjoy the various stories being read to them. *The most important part is, it needs to stand out, with bright colours and cartoon figures.*

"I've got this great idea, Paul," she says excitedly.

Paul walked in, having just made a deal with a company who specialise in royal family mementos.

"I want to set up a children's reading area. I want to call it the Babbles Children's Story Reading Group."

"Sounds interesting. Tell me more?"

"I always remember the stories you used to tell me about when you were a boy sitting in Smyths Emporium reading those books about space travel. I believe, providing we have the right place and the right person to be the storyteller, that we could have a similar thing here."

"So, I'm assuming that you want to clear off an area in here?"

"I was thinking about clearing off that space to the left. You know, the one we hardly use. I want it to have bright colours and cartoon characters."

Paul poses the hard question. "You'll need to employ a bubbly lady who's not only good at reading these stories, but who's also at making the children's experience memorable. You'll need to have the parents almost hating us because their children have nagged them into bringing them back."

Gina's frustrated comeback, "This sounds good, but just where am I going to find someone like that?"

"I believe I know just the right person,"

Gina gave Paul a questioned look.

"You remember Olivia, the sweet buxom girl with the long wavy blonde hair?"

A broad smile comes to Gina's face as she asks, "Isn't she the daughter of Colin, the man who adores my hair?"

"One and the same. We have to ask Olivia if she'd be interested in doing it, but I'm quite certain that she would agree."

Olivia the Story Reader

"I would love to be your story reader," a thrilled Olivia says when Gina rang to offer her the job.

"We still need to set the area up, but as soon as it's ready, I'll let you know."

"Looks like it's a go, but to make sure it's legal, we'll need to pass it by the various government departments."

"Well, I can handle that," Gina says. "Are you able to take care of setting up the area?"

"With pleasure, my sweet, I'm going to endeavour to give it the charm that an area like this deserves."

While Gina sorted out the many permits, Paul went out and found the best street artists that he could.

"We're going to need this place to pop. We need it to be the type of place children can't wait to come back to."

The Idea Comes to Life

In order to give the area the appeal it deserved, Paul erected a floor to ceiling screen allowing only those working on the project access.

"What on earth?" a concerned Gina asks when she walked in and saw the screen.

"It's protecting its secrecy, mi-love," Paul says as the street artists entered and walked behind the screen.

"And just who the hell are they?"

"They're part of the surprise. Believe me when I say you're going to like the end result," he says as he kissed her on the forehead.

"How's the project going?" Olivia asks Gina when she walked in and saw the screen.

"I can assume it's going well, but Paul has locked me out," a frustrated Gina says as a lady and her two children entered the emporium.

"See mummy, there's going to be all sorts of pictures on the walls," the excited child says, "and Burt told me they're going to have weekly readings of the latest comics and children's books."

Olivia looked over at Gina even more excitedly when children entered the emporium.

"Have you heard they're going to have a beautiful lady to read the stories to us," an animated girl says, "it's going to be so exciting when it's open."

"Our reputation will precede us Olivia." A delighted Gina says as even more children and their parents entered the emporium.

"The opening of the children's reading area needs to be spectacular, Olivia; we need to really show what we've got to offer."

As the street artists put the final touches to their work, and Paul finishes building his many bookcases, nervous anticipation spreads through the emporium.

"Is it finished yet?" the excited children would ask each time they entered the emporium.

"No, not yet," Gina or one of their staff members would say, "we'll put a big sign in the window telling you when it is."

As they put the final touches into place, and Paul and the street artists stood back to admire their craft, Paul turned to them and said. "I would like to thank you for your incredible work."

Around them on the walls, artists' impressions of the many story book characters sat beside well-known figures. On the floor, bright colours in a myriad of shapes and sizes invited all who entered to sit and enjoy the stories they would be told.

"We couldn't have done this without you. You have brought a plain and dreary spot to life."

"It's our pleasure," Mandy, one of artists, says. "When you first approached us to do this job, we did not know the scale. Now that it is finished, we can imagine the squeals of joy from the many children who are going to enjoy these stories."

"Care to see the finished product, my dear?"

"Of course I am. I've been waiting to see it ever since you put the screen up."

As the rest of the staff dealt with their customers, Paul walked Gina past the screen and into the reading area.

"What on earth?"

"Please don't say you don't like it."

"On the contrary, Paul, I love it. I never imagined it could look so incredible. Ours and the kids that come to have the stories read to them are going to love it," she says as she hugged him.

Buying a large piece of paper from the stationers, Gina and Paul drew shapes that resembled books around the words,

"Babbles Children's Story Reading Group starting Friday 22nd April. Bookings essential."

No sooner had they put the sign in the window than the first names appeared on the sign-up sheet.

"How many are you intending to have each time?" the parents asked.

"We're hoping to get around fifty to sixty per session, but we need to make allowances for children with special needs."

"So, how many are we actually going to allow each time?" a concerned Gina asks Paul.

"You may not realise this, but the area is modular, with special wheelchair and special need sections. My plan is we have several children each time. It's going to take a while for us to work it out."

Dressed in a beautiful floral dress with her hair hanging over her shoulders, Olivia stood out at the front of the emporium as the excited children gathered around her.

"Who wants to hear a story?" an illuminated Olivia asks as she stood amongst the excited children.

"We do!" the children yells as Olivia stepped toward the door of the emporium.

"I know you're all excited but just remember, walk do not run, and those of you in wheelchairs please don't run anyone over."

As the animated children made their way into the reading area, each finding their own place, Olivia picked up the first book.

"Looks like it's going to work out better than what we thought," Paul says as a delighted Gina watched the excited children surround Olivia as she started the first

The Grand Plan for a Colourful Future

The success of the children's reading group steadily grew over the next few years. The variety of stories and the way Olivia told them meant they were getting a greater number of children each time.

"We're going to need to get a bigger place soon if the numbers keep growing at this rate. If we get a new venue, it will need to stand out. It can't just be a carbon copy of this one. It needs to have a great degree of individuality a point of difference." Paul says to Gina.

"Why don't you buy the place next door," Gina suggests, "as we both know it's been empty for the past couple of years. It won't upset the children when we tell them we're going to be moving the reading area to a bigger place."

As Paul walked through the front door, he imagined what the interior might look like.

It needs to be divided it into separate sections, that way we can have more than one group of children here at any time. It needs to start with a reception area to allow whoever is leading to meet up with their fellow leader. If they're using one, then have the children who are here to listen to that story gather before leading them off to the section they are using.

In order to make the most of the space here, we need movable walls. We could then have a big group over there to the left, then maybe a smaller group over there to the right, or vice versa, but this means we're going to have someone responsible for all movements here, we don't want to be known as haphazard.

But the most important thing about this place is, it needs to stand out; it needs to have the sort of art that will have people talking about it for years.

Trying to imagine how the inside of the building would look, he suddenly thought about the work of M. C. Escher.

We need to have the most extraordinary art throughout the building. We need to have a place that every time someone walks in here they're going to see something new,

After finding a group of retired builders prepared to build a set of M. C. Escher inspired stairs, a nervous Paul left them to it, not knowing what the finished product would be.

He sat in his office the following afternoon, when George, the lead builder, walked in.

"We've just finished. Want to come and see the finished result?"

Walking in beside George, Paul stood there absolutely gob smacked.

Starting at the halfway point on the wall to the left, a set of upside-down facing stairs, complete with handrails, steadily made their way up to the makeshift ceiling trapdoor.

"Realising that you want this building to be one of the most remarkable around, and in keeping with the M. C. Escher theme, we built you a set of chairs."

Following George and the other builders, he was led toward a set of chairs. One of which resembled a highchair; another an old-fashioned large lounge chair; and others, when placed beside each other, gave the appearance that they were upside down.

"This is more than I could have asked. I don't know how to thank you?"

The following day, as Paul walked through the new building, he looked up to see the stairs as they travelled upside down towards the ceiling and the makeshift trapdoor.

We need to continue this theme; we cannot stop here; we need to have this as a place that blows people's minds. His thoughts deepened.

Contacting the same group of street artists that painted the original children's reading area, Paul explained to them he had bought the neighbouring property, and that he wanted it to be the most spectacular building in town.

"This needs to be a building that leaves people speechless. I want to have it filled with the type of art that almost turns people on their head to see the various paintings each time they enter."

"Sounds to me you want to follow in the path of the great M. C. Escher," Samantha, the lead street artist, says.

"I already have."

"In what way?"

"A staircase that comes out halfway up the wall, and heads to the roof upside down."

"That sounds wild," an excited Samantha says.

"We recently had a new member join us. Her name is Rachael, she's from America, and she is a specialist in doing the type of work that I believe you want. Her designs almost mirror the great M. C. Escher."

The following day, as Paul and Gina walked around the new building trying to visualise his dream, Samantha walked through the front door closely followed by an attractive lady wearing a long black dress.

Paul was immediately attracted by her beauty. Never had he seen a woman as beautiful as her before, as she smiled at him with her red made up lips as her dark hair spilled over her shoulders.

"Paul, this is the lady I told you about. Her name is Rachael. She is an expert at painting in the style of the great M. C. Escher."

"Pleased to meet you, Rachael," Paul says as he extended his hand to her.

"Likewise, Paul. I'm looking forward to using my talents to bring your reception area to life."

As Paul stood there talking to her, the aroma of her perfume reminded him of the two-hundred-dollar bottle of perfume he had bought Gina for their last anniversary.

"As you can see from the staircase leading up to the roof, I want this building to be unlike any other. I have a great appreciation for the work of M.C. Escher. Samantha has told me the finished product will be incredible."

Returning after four days of watching Rachael and a few of the other street artists enter and leave the building, Paul walked in to see a piece of art more incredible than he had ever seen before.

Beginning with the doorway, Rachael had painted a series of stylised dragons that flew from one side of the reception area to the other. Some appeared to become bigger and more colourful the further they flew. Others appeared to fly into large old-style windows that appeared to be portals into outer space.

Everywhere he looked, there was a dragon either flying across the roof or out of the window. Dragons were swooping. Others flew toward the stairs as a lady and her three children hurried themselves towards the roof, with the last dragon perched on top of the doorway.

In keeping with what Rachael had started, the other street artists painted a series of large and small creatures throughout the rest of the building. They were like those that appeared in the various stories, while others appeared to come from outer space or the artists' active imagination.

To give it a finishing touch, the words "Babbles Children's Reading Group" appeared in plain lettering on either side of the front door amongst the incredible artworks.

"This is absolutely incredible, Paul. I had no idea when you started that this would be the finished result," an awestruck Gina says as she walked through the finished building.

"My dream was to have a building unlike any other, one that would enthral and bemuse people."

"Well, you've certainly achieved that. Mossy Creek Ridge will never be the same,"

The Intergalactic Spider Cup
A Comedy

A BEAUTIFUL PRINCESS wearing an elaborate long purple dress, and a troll wearing a long coat covered in pockets bulging with currency from the surrounding planets, walks into a bar.

Surrounding them were centaurs, mermaids, warlocks and other creatures from the nearby planets all gathering together.

Two robots quickly moved up and down the bar as they served drinks to their many customers.

"Why have you brought me here tonight, Burt? It better not be another of your gambling ventures," Erin warns.

"Trust me Erin, it's not going to be like the other times. Tonight I'm going to make it big."

Since first meeting, Burt and Erin have travelled to distant planets, mixing with a variety of people, and going on adventures, many of which they have had to be rescued from.

Daughter of King Percy and Queen Alexandra, Erin has often been looked down upon because she's friends with Burt, because being a troll is seen to be the lowest of the creatures of her realm.

As the robots continued to serve their ever-growing number of customers, excited aliens gathered around the multi-striped circle in front of the bar as two spiders fought over a small piece of bread.

Scattered around the walls, creatures from the many foreign worlds stood holding wooden boxes of various sizes, each containing either a real or metal spider.

"Don't tell me you have brought me to the Spider Cup?" Erin snaps at him as Burt makes a bet with Eric the centaur.

"Didn't I tell you after the last time, when my father's soldiers had to rescue us from almost being main course for the Kraken, to never bring me to the Spider Cup again?"

"Trust me Erin, I'm on a sure thing this time," Burt pleads with confidence in his voice.

"Know this my friend, if you loose you will be walking home."

"But we live five light years from here," thinking she's joking.

Erin glared threateningly, "then I suggest you pack as many bags as you can with food, and get yourself at least one more pair of shoes, because you're in for a long walk if you lose."

"Welcome creatures from this realm and others to the Spider Cup," almost headless Gertrude says, as she floats over them.

"As you know, spiders, both metal and real will take battle this night, so make sure your bets are placed before each battle begins. We will not accept any bets after their heads have been devoured.

"Amongst the many spiders we have battling today is the massive tranatuulaiator from the forest planet of Wendor.

"During the recent battle, when humanoids tried to attack Wendor, it was found that the spiders had defeated the humanoids, penetrating their armour like nothing else had ever done. Certain parts of their anatomy, having been enlarged during battle, was used to dig the holes to bury them in."

"I'll put five hundred space credits on the tranatuulaiator," Burt says to the six-armed booky. This alarmed Erin no end.

"Five hundred! That's what you won from my father's head guard during your last game of cards. You realise he's been collecting recipes for roast and par-boiled trolls ever since.

"Relax my dear Erin, I've got this."

Excitement reins as the first battle begins.

"THE WINNER! THE MIGHTY stone spider," almost headless Gertrude announces, as the excited winners collect their spoils.

"And the winner this time, the mighty swamp spider. I think the owner of that metal spider should have known better than to attack one who can cover their opponent with slime," the announcer continues as the next match-up concludes.

"How much longer Burt, I want to be home before supper is served. Mary is serving roast sand grubs."

"It's the match after this one, just relax," Burt says infuriating Erin.

"Alright now for the main event," almost headless Gertrude says as she floats over the excited crowd.

"Can the tranatuulaiator from the forest planet of Wendor defeat the mighty metal spider?...Or will the *tough tungsten tarantula* be victorious?"

As Burt and the other excited aliens looked on, the fight started.

Using its superior size and strength, the mighty metal spider overwhelmed its slightly smaller opponent at first, but that was before it went back on its four rear legs and using its six forward legs raised itself up exposing its six large, hairy breasts.

The aliens who were in direct view now gasped in disgust and awe as the metal spider, now overwhelmed by the view, shook violently as sparks now came from its body and head, collapsing to the floor.

"I believe it is now obvious what defeated those humanoids when they tried to attack it's home world," almost headless Gertrude said, as Burt and the others who had bet on the tranatuulaiator cheered.

"Alright my friend, you won this time, but never bring me to the Spider Cup again," a frustrated Erin said as Burt fondled his winnings.

"Do you think this'll be enough to stop your father's guard from wanting to cook me?" Burt asked as he slipped five hundred credits into Erin's hand.

"Not too sure about that Burt, before we left he did ask me to try and buy lizards guts and monkeys brains, apparently they make a good marinade for roast troll."

THE NIGHT OF THE PARTY

"I'll have another barkeep," the elegantly dressed lady, wearing a black cocktail dress and makeup styled to resemble a fashion model, gracefully asked the bartender.

"But miss, this will be your fifth zombie. May I suggest you eat something?" he counsels her sternly.

Looking at him belligerently, Millie hit back, "sonny, if I wanted something to eat, I'd order something to eat. Now make me a god-damn zombie!"

Alerted by her uproar, Catherine, a lady Millie had known since they were at primary school together, approached, concerned by her demeanour.

"Why the commotion Millie? Surely things aren't that bad?" she said, trying to defuse the situation.

"Oh, you'd like to think that, wouldn't you?" Millie snapped, as she turned and glared at the bartender. "Damian, my half-wit of a boyfriend just dumped me for that tart, Julia."

"I'm sorry to hear that."

"I wish there was something I could do?"

Turning to face her, Catherine posited, "Oh, but there is. Have the bartender make you a tall drink with plenty of ice, then pretend to trip and pour it over all over Julia."

Another alerted by her uproar, Patrick, a man who has known Catherine and Millie since secondary school, approached Catherine, "Is she alright?"

"Her mongrel boyfriend just dumped her for that harpy over there."

"You mean Julia? I heard her gloating about something to her friends when I arrived. I didn't realise it was about Millie's boyfriend."

A vision of her ordering a drink with a lot of ice, then spilling it over Julia's head and down the front of her see-through blouse, now appeared in Catherine's mind.

"Do you think I should talk to her?" Patrick asked, as he looked over to see an even angrier Millie arguing with the bartender.

"If you want. Just remember what happened the night of the dance."

◇ ◇ ◇

"Look what I received in the mail?" an excited Mandy, Patrick's long-time friend, said as she ran over to meet him.

"Does it look like this?"

"You got one too,"

"So did we?" Cathy, Sean and Andrew, his other friends, said excitedly after each receiving an invitation to the local dance in the mail.

Since its beginning, the local annual dance has become the most popular social event of their small town. Held at the town hall, it has attracted bands both local and interstate, many crediting their success with performing at the dance.

As other excited teens walked through the entranceway of the town hall, Patrick and his friends arrived, hoping this was going to be a night to remember.

As Sean and Andrew spoke to two attractive women, Cathy noticed a very nervous Patrick attempting to talk to Millie, who was standing there wearing a long white dress which had an open neckline, exposing her cleavage.

Try as he might, every time he got up the nerve to speak to her, something would make him lose it, or another man would walk up and ask her to dance.

"The last dance is next. You better ask her now, you will not get another chance," Cathy said to him concerned, "I'll try to keep the other men away."

Clearing his throat and giving the appearance of self-confidence, Patrick approached her. "Would you like to dance with me, Millie?"

Looking him up and down, a conceited Millie replied, "Me dance with a loser like you are you kidding. I only dance with real men."

Shattered, Patrick stood there as Millie took to the floor with a man wearing a three-piece suit.

◇ ◇ ◇

As Millie continued arguing with the bartender, Patrick approached.

"Hey you, will you tell this excuse of a human being to give me another drink?"

"Using your charms to get what you want again, Millie? Don't you think you've had enough?"

"Who are you to tell me I've had enough?" she said as she realised who she was talking to.

"Aren't you that loser who tried to dance with me the night of the dance?"

"Yes, I am. But I will not let you intimidate me like you did that night."

"Oh, is that right!" she said with an egotistical expression on her face.

"At least I'm not getting plastered over someone who dumped me!" he said with malice.

"How dare you," she replied, her face taking on an angry red glow as she walked on shaky legs toward the door.

◇ ◇ ◇

"Look, lady, I don't have to tolerate people like you throwing up in the back seat of my car," the angry taxi driver said. "I will not be able to make any money tonight, thanks to you."

"What is this you're saying?"

"I'm not taking you any further lady," he said as he pulled up at a convenience store. "Look, it's got a wide veranda, you'll be able to stay dry under there."

"But you can't!" Millie said, as she stumbled from the taxi into the pouring rain.

Watching the taxi pull away, Millie staggered towards the convenience store, huddling from the rain under the veranda.

As other cars entered and left, Millie continued to lean against the wall of the convenience store, feeling like her life was ending.

I better get some petrol. I'm almost empty, Patrick thought as he pulled into the same convenience store.

Not realising the plight Millie was in, Patrick finished filling his car, pulling his jacket over his head as he ran toward the night window.

Putting his credit card back into his wallet, he turned and looked at the space between him and his car as the rain got even harder.

Just as he was about to pull his jacket over his head and dash through the rain, he turned and spotted Millie leaning against the convenience store wall like she was a homeless person.

"Millie, is that you? What are you doing here? I thought you got a taxi home."

"I did, but he kicked me out of his car," she said as tears poured from her eyes.

As other cars drove in and out, their headlights illuminating Millie, Patrick sat down beside her.

"What on earth has happened to you, Millie? You've gone from this assertive lass that I met the night of the dance to someone who's drinking themselves into oblivion?"

"You don't understand Patrick. I love him, and I need to come up with a way of winning him back."

Patrick sat there with a disbelieving expression on his face. "You're kidding, aren't you?"

"But I need him in my life. My life is not complete unless he's in it."

Patrick palmed his face as he thought about what she had just said.

"So, are you telling me your life is incomplete if it doesn't have a man in it?"

"Of course, it's incomplete. I don't want to be one of those losers who have no one in their life."

"Even if it means you get treated like shit?"

"My life isn't complete if it doesn't have a man in it!"

As the rain fell even harder, Patrick sat there trying to find a way of convincing Millie she didn't need a man in her life who was going to treat her like dirt.

"Buddha once said, if you find no one to support you on your journey, walk alone.

"And what does that mean?" she said with a slur, wondering what he was sai3d.

"You're a lady who believes her life is incomplete without a man in it. You're leaving yourself open to being abused by people like him, and not respected by someone who really cares about you."

"But where am I going to find a man like him?" she said in a desperate voice.

"Do you really need to ask?"

THE STORY OF A PLAY.

Let me share with you a story.

I was in my last year of school of the air education, when I was asked to be part of something special.

Growing up on my parents' durum wheat farm, I learned the key to a successful crop is knowing when to plant.

Taking care of the plants that attract the bugs that eat the bugs who would otherwise devour the crop and knowing when the best time is to harvest.

As I got older, I was allowed to assist our neighbours in milking their eighteen cows. Where I was also taught how to separate the milk and make my own butter by hand.

Like other rural children, my primary school education was conducted through the school of the air. When the satellite dish arrived, in my father's words, it became the school via computer.

Using various types of puzzles, Miss Charles, my favourite teacher, a lady who made learning English and math enjoyable, announced to her excited students, we would be putting on a production of Romeo and Juliet, or as my young sister Scarlett called it, Womeo and Oliet.

"Romeo and Juliet is a fifteenth century play written by William Shakespeare. It is a tragic love story where the two main characters, Romeo and Juliet, are supposed to be sworn enemies but fall in love.

"Because of their families' ongoing conflict, they kill themselves because they cannot cope with being separated from one another.

"As you can see, it's a very complex play, but at the same time, an exciting story.

"As well as Romeo and Juliet, we'll be looking for people to play: Mercuito, naval, Rosaline Capulet, Lady Montague, the Nurse & Friar Laurence.

"I'm going to send out a copy of all the speaking roles to your various computers. Select the one you want to play, practice as much as you can.

We will hold rehearsals in four weeks. For those who don't want to play any of these roles, we'll be looking for plenty of extras."

Walking inside, I asked my mother which role I should play?

"It's simple Alex, play the role that speaks to you the most."

Going back to my computer, I clicked on the link that said Romeo. As I read through the very complex Shakespearean language, I felt this was the role for me.

I received a lot of strange looks from the animals, as I passed them reciting some of Romeo's lines.

But, soft! What light through yonder window breaks?

It is the east, and Juliet is the sun.

Arise, fair sun, and kill the envious moon.

I even freaked out our pet sheep when I knelt in front of her and, speaking in my best Shakespearian, said.

'My love as deep; the more I give to thee, the more I have, for both are infinite.'

'Baa.'

At last, the day came to find out who would play each role.

Like a weird type of bingo, each of us was given the time we needed to log on and read for the part we wanted to play. Opening my email, I found my time was three o'clock.

Minutes felt like hours as I waited for three o'clock to come around. Finally, after what felt like the longest day in my life, my computer read 15:00.

Closing my eyes, I visualized I was walking through my neighbour's farm. Remembering the many times I had recited these lines to my neighbour's jersey cow, he said.

O, she doth teach the torches to burn bright!

It seems she hangs upon the cheek of night

As a rich jewel in an Ethiope's ear —

Beauty too rich for use, for earth too dear.

So shows a snowy dove trooping with crows,

As yonder lady omer her fellows shows.

The measure done, I'll watch her place of stand

And, touching hers, make blessed my rude hand.

Did my heart love till now? Forswear it, sight,

For I never saw true beauty till this night."

It was two very long days before we found out who had got which role.

The director was Mr Roger Davidson, a man with years of experience putting on plays for both amateur and professional actors.

"Firstly, I would like to thank all of you who read. It was great to see the level of skill you all showed.

"I realise this process has been nerve racking for you all, so without further-a-do I'm pleased to announce Madeline Davies for the role of Juliet, Alex Collins for the role of Romeo, Charles Smythe will play Mercuito, Helen Rose will play Rosaline Capulet, Sarah Thompson will play Lady Montague, Craig Lincoln will play Benvolio, Astrid Molone will play the nurse, and finally Andrew Willim's will play Friar Laurence.

"Congratulations to you all. For the rest of you, there are still roles needing to be filled."

Mum was thrilled when I told her I was going to be playing Romeo.

"Tell me, who's the girl playing Juliet?"

"It's been given to Madeline."

"Is that your attractive red head friend you're talked about?"

"Auburn, mum. She gets angry whenever anyone describes her hair as red."

"Where's it being held?"

"At the Leontine Townhall."

"But that's a two-day drive from here. Can't it be held anywhere closer?"

"It's what our director wanted. He said it's the best place to hold it. Apparently, the acoustics are incredible."

Realising we were going to be gone for a week, if not more, my parents knew someone was going to have to take care of their farm.

Dad knew Burt, his younger brother, was very reliable, so when he asked him if he could take care of the farm while they were away, he was only too happy to help.

"I'll be happy to take care of your farm. I'll bring Robert and Tim with me."

"Is that wise? If I remember, I had to rescue your sons from a gaggle of angry women the last time they were here."

"They're not like that anymore. They've both got girlfriends now."

"So, who's going to take care of your farm while you're here?"

"Debby and the girls will do that. Penny, our eldest, says she is especially capable of taking care of sheep."

It was now time for our costumes to be made.

One by one, we all stood motionless as we were measured from top to toe. Measurements were collected, bolts of various coloured material lining the walls of the warehouse that had been donated to us, brought our costumes to life by talented people.

With that done, the group photo taken, we prepared to leave.

Arriving at Leontine Townhall, many of us headed to our accommodation as Mr Davidson and his team prepared the lighting and the sound.

"Are you ready?" Madeline asked me, as Mr Davidson instructed us on the best way to deliver our roles during our final rehearsal.

"Just relax," he said, "but remember, your characters are pivotal to this entire production, the entire story."

'Thanks,' I thought as I stood there, my heart feeling as if it were about to burst out of my chest.

Turning to Madeline, I could tell from the fear in her large green eyes that she was as scared as I was.

"We're starting from where Romeo and Juliet first meet."

Remembering the hours I had spent walking through the fields practicing my lines, I blocked Mr Davidson and his crew from my mind, and putting my attention on Madeline, delivered my lines in the way I had practiced, when I had substituted Madeline for one of my neighbours cows.

Silence filled the hall. As Mr Davidson and his team faced us, their expressions were like stone.

Like a loud crack of thunder, Mr Davidson's assistant, Molly, raised her hands, and began to applaud. The rest enthusiastically joined in.

Romeo and Juliet

The Leontine Townhall

1 Performance only

"I'm flabbergasted," Mr Davidson said as the applause continued, "to think, you received these words via a computer and practiced in fields away from the rest of the cast, yet you delivered a performance that puts those who perform in grand halls and before millions of people to shame.

Never had I felt as nervous as I felt that night as I stood there, my opening lines going through my mind.

As the other actors and actresses necessary for act one prepared, the curtain slowly rose.

Changing into my impressive fifteenth century outfit, I prepared for the wedding scene.

As the other actors and actresses gathered, Madeline, adorned in a resplendent sixteenth century bridal gown, strolled with unwavering poise towards us, her confidence overwhelming me.

As I walked onto the stage, an overwhelming mixture of love, longing and fear surged through me as I prepared to speak words of love to a lady I had ever only considered a friend.

Romeo
Ah, Juliet, if the measure of thy joy
Be heaped like mine and that thy skill be more
To blazon it, then sweeten with thy breath
This neighbour air, and let rich music's tongue
Unfold the imagined happiness that both
Receive in either this dear encounter.

The heartbreaking end of our story had arrived.

We were acutely aware of Mr Davidson's high expectations, but as I lay deceased on the floor. The sound of stifled sobs reverberated throughout the theatre.

Finally, it was done.

As the cast assembled and the sound of applause rung out, we turned to each other and smiled.

Turning to Madeline I smiled, "We did it

THE SIDECAR CUP

a story told in reverse

Olivia trembled as she remembered incident.

"Good morning, ladies and gentlemen, and welcome to the last and ultimate day of the Isle of Man Sidecar Cup.

Two days ago, we witnessed Olivia and Mia aboard the Silver Bandit set a new lap record.

Those of you who were here yesterday witnessed the spectacular two-bike challenge, our congratulations to Frank and Michael Redding aboard the Green Flash for being the eventual winners, our sympathies go to Greg and Michael aboard the Red Baron who were involved in that unfortunate incident with Olivia and Mia aboard the Silver Bandit: it is suspected that Greg is going to be left a quadriplegic."

The scuff marks leading up from the fairing reminded Olivia of yesterday's accident. As she stood there, memories of seeing the Red Baron as it attempted to overtake them, the bang, then skidding on its nose, left her with trepidation.

"Are you ready for today's race?" Patricia, the crew boss, asked.

"I'm not sure I'm able to race today," she said.

"I remember seeing you flip your bike in the kitty litter at Phillip Island Mia, being thrown from the chair, and your bike lying upside down. I then remember seeing you dragging the bike free, righting it, throwing Mia back on and winning the race."

"But that was different!"

"How was it different? You did nothing wrong. The accident was his fault. Never forget that."

"It's now time, ladies and gentlemen; can the team of Olivia Holt and Mia Sparrow aboard the Silver Bandit win the coveted title and be crowned the Isle of Man Sidecar Cup champions," the announcer proclaimed as the excited crowd swelled.

Sliding on her helmet, Olivia assumed her position as Mia climbed aboard. Waiting nervously, Olivia's heart pounded as she waited for the light to turn green.

Spinning the drive tyre, Mia hung on as Olivia took off from the start line. Maintaining the speed that had given them the track record, they sped through the first corner, clicking down a gear. They both held on as the bike went momentarily airborne.

Left.

Right.

Left.

Right

The corners came as Mia struggled to keep the bike on the ground, burying herself behind the fairing she held on as they sped at full speed toward the hairpin.

With her elbow almost touching the ground, Mia held on as Olivia manoeuvred the bike through the hairpin. Coming out of the bend, she again tucked her head below the fairing as Olivia sped up the back straight.

Sounding like a scourge of mosquitoes, the bike raced down the final straight as the surrounding crowd cheered. Noticing the clock on the approach to the finish line, Olivia smiled when she realised they had set another track record.

"They've done it, ladies and gentlemen. Never in the history of the Sidecar Cup has the track record been beaten not once. But twice! We now wait to see if David and Sebastian aboard the Black Magic can better their time and steal first place,"

Holding each other tightly by the hand, Olivia and Mia watch the clock as team Black Magic sped around the track.

"Here they come, ladies and gentlemen. Can they do it? Can they grab first place? No, Olivia and Mia and team Silver Bandit have done it. For the first time, an all-ladies' team has won the Isle of Man Sidecar Cup!!!!"

"Salutations and welcome to the two-bike challenge, "Gabrielle, the two-bike challenge official, announced to the assembled teams."

"As we all know, yesterday Olivia and Mia from Australia set a new lap record. We're not interested in things like that today, the only thing we're interested in is, who can beat their competitor in the fastest time, because the team with the fastest time will be pronounced the winner. By now, you should all have been handed an envelope. it contains the number of the team you are going to be racing against."

A look of loathing was clear on Olivia's face as she read who they would be racing against.

"You don't look happy, Olivia? Mia asks as Olivia hands her the sheet with their competitor's name on it.

"Oh, you've got to be kidding!?"

"I'm afraid not. We're up against Greg and Michael Perkins."

"Those arrogant bastards, we better make sure we put them in their place."

"Ready to be humiliated, ladies?" An arrogant Greg Perkins asked as he walked into their pit.

"Don't worry about us. You just make sure you stay out of our way."

"It will not be like yesterday. Today you're competing against a real team."

"Is that what you call yourselves? I didn't see your bike getting anywhere near ours yesterday."

"That's because we're waiting for tomorrow. That's when they'll see a real bike in action."

"If you don't mind, please return to your own pit," an annoyed Patricia said. "My girls need to get ready."

"It's all set. I've set the gears, the chains are tightened, the rest is up to you," Leonard, their chief mechanic said, as he wiped his grease-stained face and hands with a rag.

"Now for the ultimate grudge match, ladies and gentlemen, will the Red Baron, with pilot Greg Perkins leave the Silver Bandit with pilot Olivia Holt in its wake, or are we going to see a demonstration of female superiority? only time will tell."

Sitting nervously on the start line, Olivia waited as the Red Baron rolled up beside her. Knowing that this was not just a battle of the sexes, she prepared to give it her all.

"Keep it clean and keep it safe. We all want to race tomorrow," the race official said, preparing for the race to start.

Nervous tension filled the surrounding area as both drivers revved their engines, their passengers preparing for the off. With their eyes fixed on the lights, they shot off from the line.

Showing the speed of her bike and her skills as a driver, Olivia rounded the corner in first place. Around them, spectators cheer as both bikes sped past them, jostling for position.

Reaching her maximum speed, Olivia rushed down the main straight, hoping to be in a good position as they approach Mulligan's Corner. As Mia tucked herself in, Olivia made the turn.

Just as Olivia thought she had gotten through the corner cleanly, there was a sudden flash of red as both bikes came together, unsure of what had just happened, Olivia and Mia hung on as their bike was pushed to the side, as the Red Baron skidded past them on its nose, as Michael slid down the track on his back.

Coming to their senses, Mia and Olivia were shocked to see the Red Baron on the other side of the track, its wheels facing upward, fearing that Greg was badly injured. They ran across the track.

"Careful there, hold his neck, we don't want to see him falling," the chief ambulance officer said as the other officer pulled the stretcher from the ambulance.

As Olivia, Mia, and the safety marshals lifted the bike, two other safety marshals slid under the bike, slipping the neck brace around Greg's neck, lifting it higher, both ambulance officers slid him from the bike, placing him on the stretcher.

With the track clear and Olivia and Mia having returned to the pit with their bike, the racing resumed.

"Our congratulations to Frank and Michael Redding aboard Green Flash, winner of the two-bike challenge," the excited announcer said.

"Further congratulations go to team Black Mamba and team Yellow Canary for setting the next two fastest times."

"Oh, thank you, I'll tell her." Olivia heard Patricia said, as she finished her call.

"Tell me what?"

"Now I don't want you to feel that you're responsible, but as a result of the accident it is suspected that Greg is going to be left a quadriplegic."

"Oh, no! are they sure there is nothing they can do?"

"It's suspected that the combination of the impact, and the fact that the bike was resting on his head, will leave him with a very serious neck injury that could lead to quadriplegia."

As Olivia remembered the accident, she reviewed the day that led up to it.

"Welcome ladies and gentlemen, to this year's Isle of Man Sidecar Cup.

It's thrilling to see so many local and international teams. I believe we even have one team from Australia.

The Sidecar Cup isn't just a multi-day points race, although day one and day three are, day two is when we hold the separate two-bike challenge where we will match you up with another team, it is the most thrilling, and indeed the most dangerous of all three days with the winners securing the two-bike challenge cup.

For those of you who have raced here before, you know that this is one of the most spectacular race circuits in the world, indeed it is the only strictly road circuit around, for those of you who have never raced here before, you are in for one hell of an experience."

"Where might you be from?" Richard asked in a very proper English accent.

"We're from Australia. Where are you from?" Olivia asked in a girlish tone as she wound her finger through her hair.

"My wife Emma and I are from Cornwall."

"Have you raced here before?"

"Emma and I have raced here for the last five years. We3 won the sidecar cup on our first try, but since then faster, more high-tech bikes have seen us relegated to around eighth or tenth."

"Spiffy bike you've got there," Richard said as he watched it being rolled out of its trailer.

"Thank you."

"I'm not sure if you've heard, but word about the Silver Bandit being crewed by an all-female team is spreading," Paul, one of the crew leaders, said.

"They're saying that an all-ladies team hasn't got what it takes to win around here," Ian his friend said.

"Is that so?"

As the bike was pushed to the start line, Olivia and Mia walked up behind it as they slipped on their helmets.

"Just remember it's just another race. I know what you're capable of and so do you. Don't forget what you did to get here.

"The first lap is your practice lap, then it starts in earnest, watch out for Mulligan's bend, I've been told it can catch out even a seasoned team," Patricia said before standing beside the safety barrier as Olivia was waved off.

Heading down the straight, Olivia sped as fast as she dare as the first corner approached. Leaning across the bike, Mia hung onto the far-side handhold as Olivia deftly manoeuvred through the corner.

It was then a mixture of grabbing onto the far-side handhold, then the near-side handhold as Olivia sped through the succession of right-handed, followed by left-handed corners.

Approaching Mulligan's corner, Olivia selected what she hoped was the right gear. Mia suddenly realised what had caused the other teams to crash as a large concrete wall charged at them, causing her to gear down and lifting the passenger-side wheel, Olivia steered the bike through the corner, placing the wheel down, Mia tucked herself below the fairing as they continued down the next straight.

Finding themselves travelling along the first part of the exposed straight, they knew the hairpin was next. Leaning out as far as she dare, and with her elbow almost scraping on the ground, Mia held on as Olivia navigated through the hairpin.

With the track now familiar to them, and the memory of Mulligan's corner still fresh in both their minds, they headed out on their first official lap.

Riding like they did on the Australian tracks, their name started appearing higher and higher up the score sheet, as the other teams looked on.

Knowing the finish line was only four corners away, they sped as fast as they could risk, crossing the finish line a full two seconds faster than the second fastest team.

"I didn't believe it was possible ladies and gentlemen, but Olivia and Mia aboard the Silver Bandit are not only in first place, but have set a new track record in doing so. Is there another team capable of beating them? We will not know this until next we race in two days' time, the excited announcer said as reporters and camera crews rushed the girls.

"Did you think you could set a new track record when you first arrived?"

"Our only thought was racing on this incredible track. It's unlike any we have raced on before."

"So can I tell from the accent that you're from Australia?"

"Yes, we are."

"We're going to be the team to set the fastest time, not a lady's team from Australia," the arrogant man said as he walked into their pit.

"You think you can do better than us?" Olivia asked in a conceited tone as she turned and faced him.

"The name's Greg, and this is my baby brother, Michael. We've won on every circuit throughout Europe, setting lap records on half of them."

"But have you ever raced in Australia? Mia and I have run and won on circuits far riskier than any European circuit. Ever heard of Mount Panorama? It's a mountain circuit. We set the lap record on our last race there. You think you're better than us? Let's see it!" Olivia smirked.

"You might have beaten us today, but you will not better us on the two-bike challenge. That trophy has already got our name on it," Greg said, as they left the pit.

Arriving at the track, Olivia entered the pit to see her naked bike sitting there, the mechanics leaning across it as they put the final touches to the engine and suspension.

With the tyres inflated, and the body bolted on, they prepared for the race to start, hoping that a win today would send them from the familiar tracks of Australia all the way to the Isle of Man.

"Good afternoon, ladies and gentlemen, and welcome to the final and deciding round to see which of you will be heading to the Isle of Man to compete in the Isle of Man Sidecar Cup. At the moment, Olivia and Mia are leading the score sheets, but a win today will secure them the right to compete." Peter, the manager of the Three Wheel Bandits, announces to the assembled crowd.

"Today we will be racing around the rather tricky Winton circuit, which, as you all know has many complicated corners to it. Race clean, obey the rules, and if you blow a tyre, for hell's sake get off the track."

"Well, this is it. Our dream is only a few corners away," Mia said as the arrogant driver of the Orange Menace pulled up beside them.

"That's unless I cross the finish line first. You realise Doug and I0 are only twenty points behind you and the winner gets a hundred points today."

"You just keep your orange sludge away from me," Olivia answered.

"Mia and I are the ones destined to race at the Isle of Man. and you know it. Your only chance of getting over there is if I sell you my bike, which will never happen." Olivia said as she slid on her helmet.

Taking their place on the second row, it didn't take long for the jostling to start. Riding as cautiously as she dare, Olivia weaved her way through the traffic as Mia and the other passengers leapt from side to side, keeping their bikes safely on the track.

Nearing the halfway point, Olivia turned onto the main straight as she passed the last bike between them and victory. With the track now clear of other bikes, she sped down the main straight, knowing that only a catastrophe would stop them from getting to the Isle of Man.

Catching a glimpse of the many signs held by their supporters, Olivia sped down the back straight. Using their unique cornering skills, they rode ever faster through the tricky six corner chicane, as other teams landed in the safety gravel.

With only one lap remaining and no other team near them, Olivia and Mia gave their supporters a thrill as they let the passenger wheel lift as they sped through the corners.

Speeding down the main straight for the last time, they raised their arms in triumph as the crowd around them cheered.

Standing on the first-place dais, memories of the accident and the subsequent injuries to Greg made being handed the trophy hard for Olivia.

As they walked back to the pit, Patricia smiled when she saw Michael enter.

"Don't blame yourself for yesterday's accident, Olivia. If my brother hadn't been racing like a fool, and had held back, the accident would never have happened.

A look of relief replaced the visible guilt that had been on Olivia's face.

"Thank you, Michael. By the way, how is he?"

"As best as can be expected. Though he's still angry that he can't race today."

Bibliography
Actual motor racing circuits used in this story
Isle of Man
Mount Panorama
Winton

Philip Island

About the Author

Losing his job just before covid struck, Mark joined U3A where he learned from not only his instructors but his fellow authors the joy of writing,

Exploring the challenges of writing stories of various lengths have led to a world where he tells stories in his own unique way.

www.ingramcontent.com/pod-product-compliance
Lightning Source LLC
Chambersburg PA
CBHW071229130726
47998CB00002B/888